P9-CEV-403

F

Perpetrated by LESLIE TRYON

ALBERT'S HALLOWEEN

The CASE of the STOLEN PUMPKINS

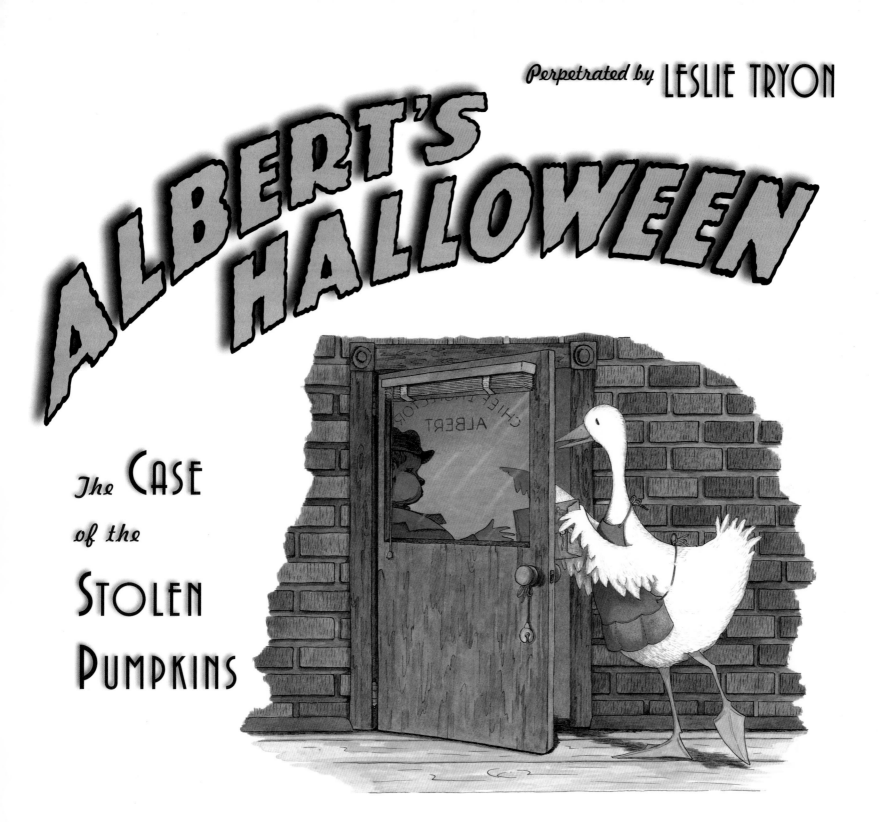

ATHENEUM BOOKS for YOUNG READERS

East Bridgewater Public Library
Children's Room
32 Union Street
East Bridgewater, MA 02333

Investigation
assisted by:
MARY D. LANKFORD and
CONRAD PEDERSON

Atheneum Books for Young Readers
An imprint of Simon & Schuster
Children's Publishing Division
1230 Avenue of the Americas
New York, New York 10020

Copyright © 1998 by Leslie Tryon
All rights reserved, including the right of reproduction in whole or in part in any form.

Book design by Michael Nelson

The text of this book is set in Cosmos
Printed in Hong Kong
First Edition
10 9 8 7 6 5 4 3 2 1
Library of Congress Cataloging-in-Publication Data:
Tryon, Leslie.
Albert's Halloween: The Case of the Stolen Pumpkins / written and
illustrated by Leslie Tryon.—1st ed.   p.   cm.
Summary: Chief Inspector Albert the Duck and his three
detective assistants follow a series of clues to find the batch
of pumpkins stolen from the town pumpkin patch.
ISBN 0-689-81136-5 (alk. paper)
1. Pumpkin—Fiction. 2. Halloween—Fiction.
3. Ducks—Fiction. 4. Mystery and
detective stories.
I. Title.   PZ7.T7865Amh 1998
[E]—dc21
97-45007

Happy Halloween Birthday
J. RILEY "DAD" FOWLER

THE CASE OF
THE STOLEN PUMPKINS

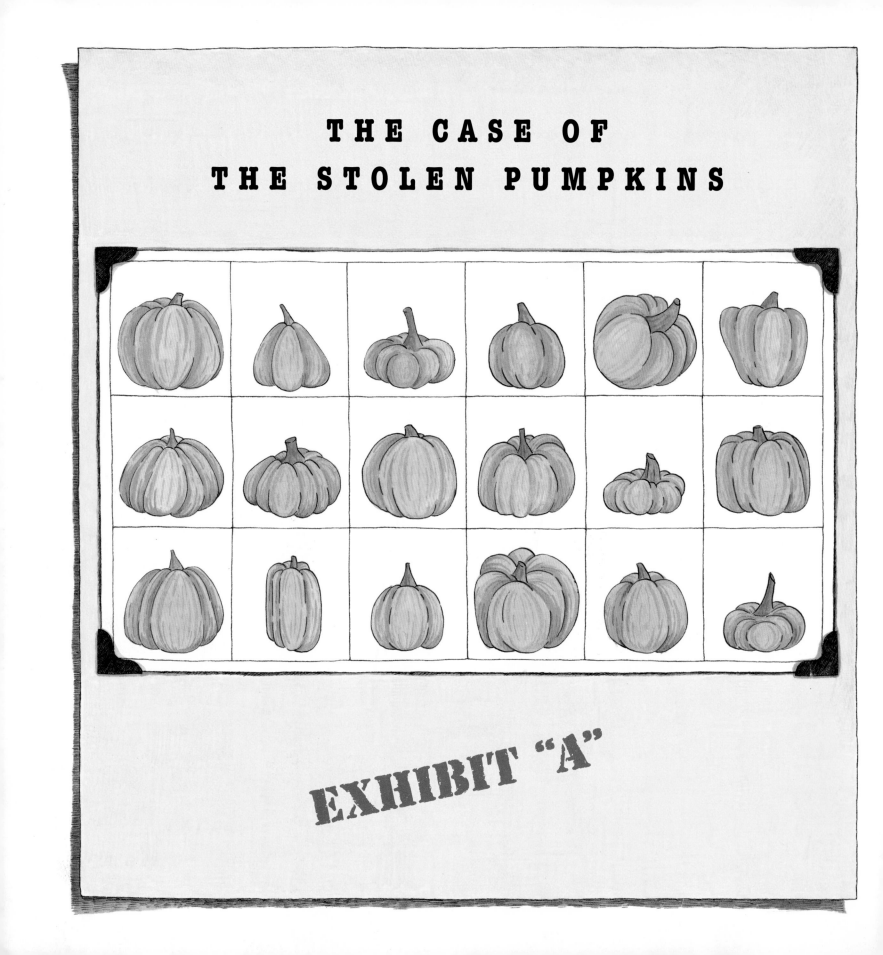

EXHIBIT "A"

October 31st, 5:00 p.m.

Miss Maple, Shamrock Homes, and Sam Slade, please come quickly. Meet me in Patsy Pig's Pleasant Valley Pumpkin Patch. I've learned from an unidentified source that all the pumpkins shown in Exhibit "A" have been stolen.

It could be a trick. Our job? Elementary! We must find the pumpkins, return them to the pumpkin patch, and catch the thief before any jack-o'-lanterns can be carved or trick-or-treating can begin.

Chief Inspector Albert

TOP PRIORITY

Chief Inspector Albert and the three detectives spread out around the pumpkin patch and get right to work. They leave no pumpkin leaf unturned in their search for clues.

Sam is the first to find something. "Over here. I found a note!"

PATSY'S PLEASANT VALLEY PUMPKIN PATCH

closed

Sam's light flashes on a mysterious message
written on a paper bag. They read every word,
very carefully.

"Extraordinary!" Miss Maple remarks. "The
scarecrows all appear to be scary and somewhat
crooked. Wherever shall we begin?"

Your pumpkins can't just disappear
But Where are they?

They are not here.

18 pumpkins were bagged by me,
All but 1 as you now will see.

I hid it near the scariest crow,
The crooked one with the
pipe elbow.

They search every scarecrow, looking for the pumpkin mentioned in the note.

Finally Miss Maple calls out, "I found the pipe elbow."

At that very same moment Albert discovers a piece of pink paper tucked into the scarecrow's right shoe, and a pumpkin next to it.

"Elementary," Albert remarks. "The thief hopes to throw us off the trail by teasing us with one of the pumpkins as well as another clue."

"What does it say?" asks Miss Maple

Where books are standing, row on row,
Between the stone heads you must go.
I think I've heard the lions roar.
But the raven still squawks, Nevermore!
If you hurry
you might just catch
me
and the missing
pumpkin patch

They know that the place "where books are standing, row on row," must be the library. But when they arrive there they see neither a thief nor the missing pumpkins.

"I sense a pattern developing," says Miss Maple.

"Yes," Sam says, "two notes and one pumpkin so far. I'll bet we find another pumpkin."

Miss Maple picks up a strand of pumpkin vine at the top of the steps.

A moment later Albert and Sam discover another pumpkin lying in plain sight. One thing is obvious—the pumpkin thief has been here and gone. Now there are sixteen left to find. But why has the pumpkin thief left two pumpkins for them to find so easily?

Meanwhile, Shamrock is on to something. He remembers the clue about the lions' roar. . . .

There is a tree that's standing still,
Though it is dead it has its fill
Of things that hoot and crawl and creep
At night, while you are fast asleep.

Inside the burned-out hole is where
you'll find surprises,
IF YOU DARE!

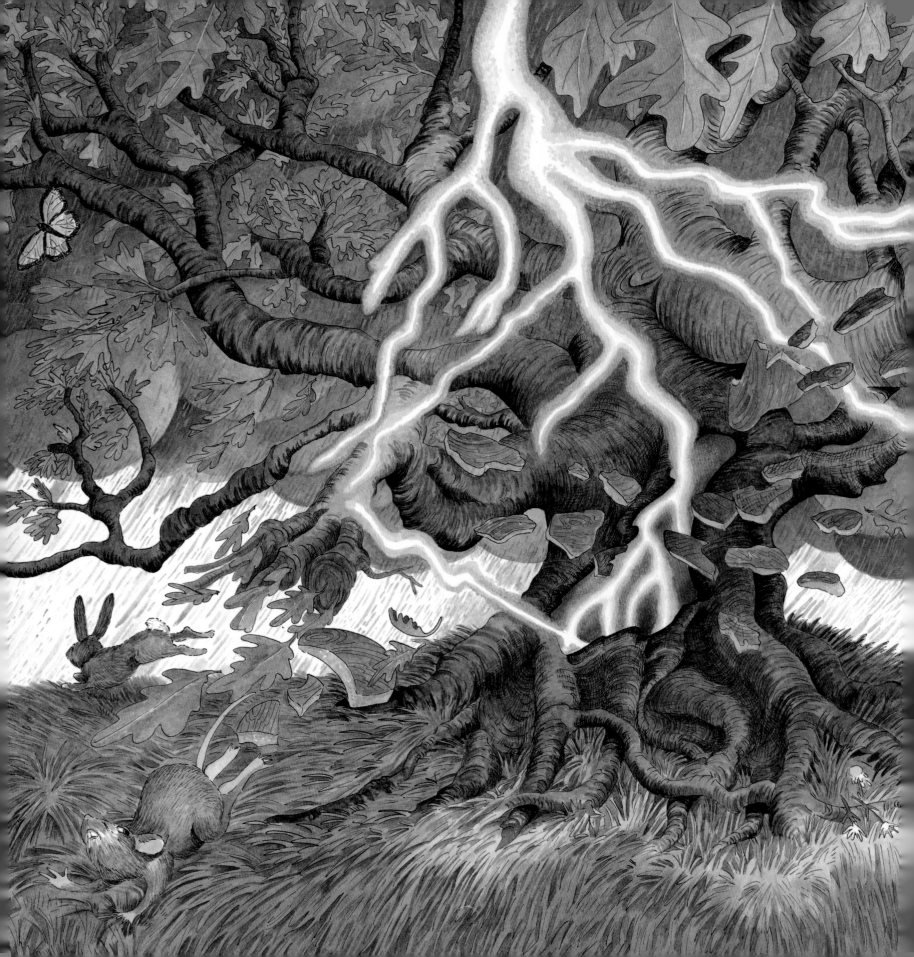

Flashback: Long ago, it was a beautiful tree. But during the worst storm in Pleasant Valley history, a bolt of lightning sliced a huge hole in the trunk. A smoldering red glow from that hole could be seen long afterward. Now this dead tree is home to the creatures of the night.

Chief Inspector Albert and the detectives race along the dark country road, past the witch-cap trees, around the haunted meadow, and up the knoll to the old dead tree. But who will actually reach into the spooky dark hole to see what's there?

Only Albert can reach up that high. Sam, Shamrock, and especially Miss Maple are all very grateful that they cannot. Inside the hole Albert finds an odd, twisted piece of green paper with writing on it, hanging at the very top. Next to the twisted piece of paper, resting against the tree trunk, is another pumpkin and a small black velvet bag tied with an orange ribbon.

"Curious," says Miss Maple.

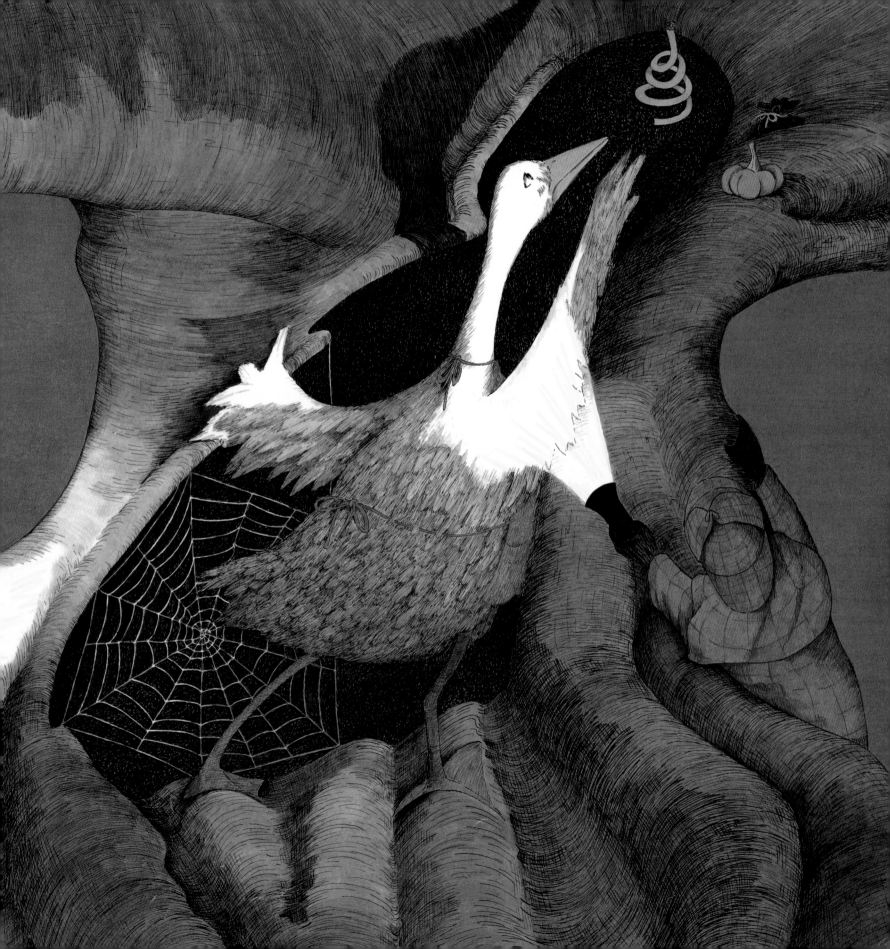

They find a spot away from the tree and
gather in a tight circle around the note.

Inside the black velvet bag they find no clue, just one ordinary brass key.

"It's time to look carefully at these clues again," insists Miss Maple. "There must be a key to the key."

"We seem to be very good at finding notes, but what about the other fifteen pumpkins?" asks Sam.

"Elementary," Chief Inspector Albert says. "Somewhere there is a lock that this key fits."

"But where?" asks Shamrock.

Finally, a door opens.

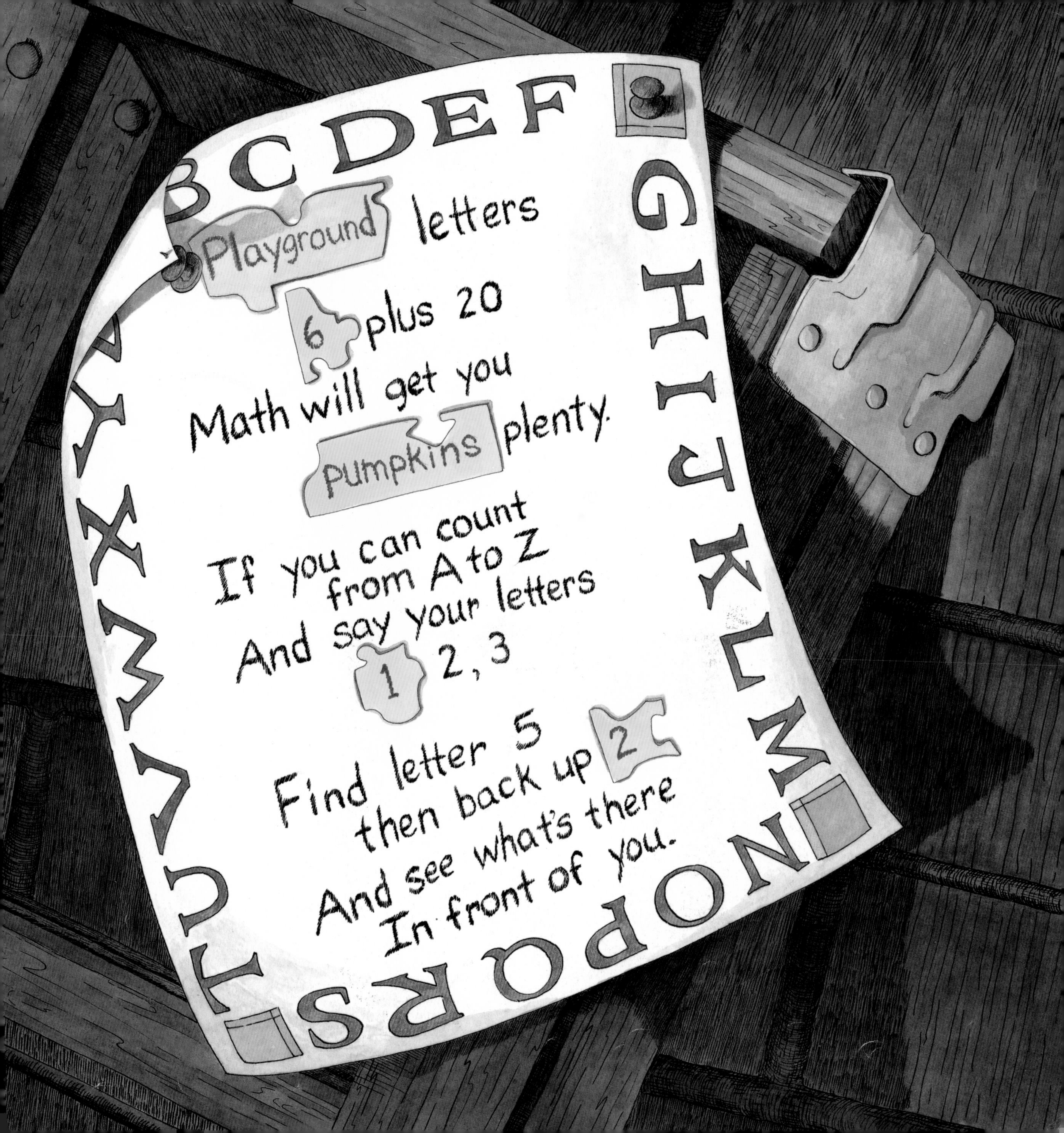
BCDEF
GHIJKLM
NOPQRS
TUVWXY
Playground letters
6 plus 20
Math will get you
pumpkins plenty.
If you can count
from A to Z
And say your letters
1 2, 3
Find letter 5
then back up 2
And see what's there
In front of you.

"Count from A to Z? Say your letters, 1, 2, 3?" Shamrock says. "What kind of gibberish is that, anyway?"

Chief Inspector Albert suggests that it might be a code. "'Back up' probably means minus: If E is the fifth letter of the alphabet, then that would mean A, B, C equals 1, 2, 3."

"That's right," says Sam, who is very good at math. "E minus 2 is C. We must go to the letter C." At the letter C they find another clue and another pumpkin.

This is the spot where
my game ends,
And the real pumpkin hunt begins.

Now you must retrace your path.
Work the puzzle. Do the math.

4 little pumpkins

you got for free

The other 14 you just didn't see.
Every word I wrote, you read.
Now RED words
should be read instead.

Miss Maple takes all the clue notes from her purse and spreads them out on the grass. Carefully they remove each of the red words from the notes. Finally they put the last puzzle piece in place and then read the message:

"So!" Sam says. "The pumpkins weren't really stolen after all."
"That's right, it's a game," says Miss Maple. "Very clever indeed."
"But who would make up a game like this?" Shamrock asks.
"I know who," Albert says. "It's really quite elementary."
And so, with the puzzle assembled, Chief Inspector Albert, Miss Maple, Sam Slade, and Shamrock Homes retrace their route to find the rest of the pumpkins and return them to Patsy's Pumpkin Patch.

They found the pumpkins. *Can you?*

THE CASE OF
THE STOLEN PUMPKINS
PUMPKIN PATCH
PUMPKIN PATCH
FREE
PUMPKIN PATCH
PUMPKIN PATCH
DEAD TREE
DEAD TREE
LIBRARY
PLAYGROUND
DEAD TREE
FREE
PLAYGROUND
DEAD TREE
DEAD TREE
FREE
DEAD TREE
PATSY
FREE
EXHIBIT "A"

October 31st, 7:00 p.m.

Just as I surmised, the one who tricked us was none other than Patsy Pig herself, the proprietor of the Pumpkin Patch. It was Patsy who wrote the notes and it was she who hid the pumpkins. It was Patsy's game all along.

Disguised in a shrub costume she made herself, Patsy was apprehended at 6:58 p.m. She had in her possession the last of the missing pumpkins.

Chief Inspector Albert

CASE CLOSED